Nathaniel Hawthorne, Elizabeth Weller Peck

Nathaniel Hawthorne's Scarlet Letter

Nathaniel Hawthorne, Elizabeth Weller Peck

Nathaniel Hawthorne's Scarlet Letter

ISBN/EAN: 9783337343484

Printed in Europe, USA, Canada, Australia, Japan

Cover: Foto ©Andreas Hilbeck / pixelio.de

More available books at **www.hansebooks.com**

NATHANIEL HAWTHORNE'S

SCARLET LETTER,

DRAMATIZED.

A PLAY IN FIVE ACTS.

BY

ELIZABETH WELLER

BOSTON:
FRANKLIN PRESS: RAND, AVERY, & CO.
1876.

THE SCARLET LETTER.

DRAMATIS PERSONÆ.

HESTER PRYNNE, Wife of Roger Chillingworth.
ARTHUR DIMMESDALE, Clergyman.
ROGER CHILLINGWORTH, Doctor.
PEARL, Daughter of Hester Prynne.
REV. JOHN WILSON.
GOVERNOR BELLINGHAM.
Countrymen, Citizens, Witch, Beadle, and Jailer.

ACT I.

SCENE I. — *The Stage represents the front of Boston Prison in early Colonial times. Men and women stand waiting (one with an infant in her arms) till the Beadle shall herald* HESTER'S *coming.*

DAME LAWTON.

I 'm hearty; thanks, good neighbor.
I walked me to the town :
'Tis rare such sights to see, else I'd not come.
We women of the country, who thriftly labor,
Can but wonder that any woman findeth time to sin :

It proveth well the adage true, —
" That Satan findeth work for idle hands to do."

DAME HERNDON.

True, true; and yet there be
Some who claim her never idle.   Her defty fingers
Did dainty broideries do, that she bestowed in charity ;
And soft-hearted folk do hold it forth
In palliation, that she be not entirely wrong,
And come not here to see her taste
The bitter fruit her hand did gather.
My man, in effort to dissuade, in anger grew,
And rated soundly that women gloried in dishonor.
I glory that justice be done.
Would that my will the punishment might give !
I'd hold the law clean to the text,
And hang the woman 'twixt heaven and earth.

DAME FALES.

[*A young wife with baby in her arms, laying
her hand on* DAME HERNDON's *plead-
ingly, and interrupting her.*]

Be not so wroth !   Some pity show !
My breast, which bears my first-born's tender weight,
Can pity this unblest maternity.

DAME HERNDON.

Ay !   But thou wert ever a tender-hearted wench,
And in your own white purity

Didst slowly credit Mistress Hester's shame :
Her child shrieked out her black dishonor
Ere thou a censure didst bestow.   E'en then you wept
    to blame.

DAME FALES.

I could but weep: [*clasping her baby tenderly*]
Motherhood to me such sweet joys gave
That I can pity one who holdeth in dishonor
The crowning glory of a woman's life.
Ay, my deepest soul with sorrow keen is stirred.
This moment I could weep; but tears disturb
The nurse my pretty babe doth claim :
For him I do refrain.

DAME HERNDON.

Thy pity I can well respect ;
But in my soul I do despise
The mercy of these God-fearing magistrates,
Who will not brand a face that God made fair,
Nor break a neck made white and long.
Had Mistress Hester been but plain,
The law would not have felt this strain,
And honest women been avenged.
Our old code did read, To death the adulteress give :
Why spare this pretty mistress ?

DAME BOND.

I'll tell you a piece of my mind : —
Greatly for the public weal, that we of mature years,

Church-members all of good repute,
Into such hands the law should give
The judgment of such malefactress.
We bear the reputation of our sex:
'Tis meet its punishment bestow.

HUSBAND OF DAME BOND.

Ye have more to forgive than sin:
She hath beauty and youth for her blame:
My good wife won't forget, — not she!

DAME BOND.

What think ye, women? —
Would Mistress Hester move our pity more
That she be fair? Beauty maketh men so merciful!
It shall not touch our hearts.
All womanhood one voice should cry, —
Death, death, to the adulteress!

DAME HERNDON.

Thou speakest rightly. A wholesome fear of the
        gallows
Tends much to strengthen woman's purity.

TOWNSMAN.

Out upon thee for a defamer of thy sex!
Has woman no purity save that which springs
From fear of death or shame?
Must we be taught by woman
That pure womanhood, from love of soul-cleanness, be
        dead?

DAME HERNDON.

Nay, nay! thou art too fast.
But I'm aweary of this disputation.
Even as my soul's aweary, so is my body:
I've waited since the sun uprose.
Why comes she not? Shall honest people patient
    stand
While infamy shall deck itself?

TOWNSMAN.

Ay, gossip! hold thy tongue:
She quickly comes.   Your deepest malice
Scarce could wish her punishment more keen
Than through the hateful, sneering crowd to tread,
Bearing on breast and arm the symbol and proof of
    shame.
O woman! that bravely bears and dies
For love and faith, know not one pang
Of pity and regret when shame upon
A sister's face is set.

SCENE II. — *The prison door opens.* HESTER *comes
out bearing her babe upon her arm ; on her breast
a Scarlet Letter, ornamented. The Beadle her-
alds her coming.*

BEADLE.

Make way, make way! in our good king's name.
I promise you all, both men and women,
And children small, a sight of her brave attire.

2

Till the midday sun shall shine
In the market-place shall stand
Mistress Prynne, her babe, and her Scarlet Letter.
A blessing on this righteous colony, Massachusetts!
— So come along!

DAME HERNDON.

                    Saw you ever such brazenness?
The hussy to flaunt in the face of our magistrates
Her shame as an ornamentation!

DAME BOND.

I'd have her gown so fine stripped off
Her dainty shoulders, and raiment coarse instead.
In place of her scarlet beauty,
My old rheumatic flannel should tell
How worthless her reputation.

DAME HERNDON.

But she has stitched and stitched
It cunningly, in truth.
She makes a worship of her degradation.
She merits well her garments torn,
Her back well lashed, till ribbed its whiteness.

DAME BOND.

She does bravely wear it.

DAME FALES.

Oh, peace, good neighbors, peace!
Not so loud! Misery makes the hearing clear.
Not one stitch in all that fancy broidered letter
But struck her soul in agony.

SCENE III. — HESTER *mounts the scaffold. Crowd of people look on. A stranger accompanied by an Indian approaches, and stands with the crowd. He lays his hand on a townsman's shoulder, and points his finger in inquiry at* HESTER.

ROGER.

Good sir, who is this woman, pray?
And wherefore set to public shame?

TOWNSMAN.

You needs must be a stranger in these parts,
If you know not of Mistress Hester Prynne,
And of her evil doing.
A heavy scandal hath she raised,
And sorely tried the flock of goodly Master Dimmesdale.
     [*Scanning him closely, and his Indian companion.*

ROGER CHILLINGWORTH.

I am a stranger, — you truly speak, —
And wander 'gainst my will;
Grievous mishaps by sea and land;
Held long in bondage 'mong heathen folks,
Till from the southward hither brought
     [*Motions towards the Indian.*
To be redeemed from my captivity.
But tell me of this woman,
Of her offences.   Detail, sparing nought.

E'en though my soul it sicken,
And rend the faith I held in woman.
Speak, man and friend: an eager listener I.

TOWNSMAN.

Methinks your heart it gladdens,
From perils freed, to reach a land where sin is pun-
    ished
In sight of rulers and of people.
Ay! brave New England holds a godly people,
Whose hands do quickly grasp at justice.
Yonder woman, wedded to a certain learned man,
English by birth, did live in Amsterdam.
Some time agone he minded to cross him over,
And cast his lot with us of Massachusetts.
Necessary affairs compelled him to remain,
His wife preceding him,
And dwelling 'mong us for two years past.
No tidings came of this learned gentleman.
His wife, look you!
Being to her own misguidance.

ROGER.

Ah! ah! I conceive you.
By your favor, sir, who may the father be
Of yonder babe?

TOWNSMAN.

Of the truth, my friend, that remaineth still a riddle.
The Daniel that shall expound is still a-wanting.

Madam Hester's firm proud lips have not parted,
And at their silence sorely are the magistrates taxed.
Peradventure even now the guilty one
Looks on this spectacle
Unknown, unshunned, and uncondemned of men,
Oblivious that God sees, and retribution cometh
For sins that lie bitter to his conscience unconfessed.

ROGER.

The learned man should come
To look into this mystery.

TOWNSMAN.

It behooves him well — if still in life.
Our Massachusetts magistracy
Bethink themselves that she were young and fair,
And tempted in her fall.
The extremity of our righteous law,
And penalty thereof, is death.
In their mercy, and great tenderness,
They doomed this Mistress Prynne
To stand for five hours upon the platform of the
        pillory,
And then, and ever after the remainder of her life,
To wear the mark of shame upon her breast.

ROGER.

A wise sentence.
Thus she will ever be a living sermon
On the sin that stamped her bosom's scarlet in.

It irks me much, the partner of her guilt
Stands not on yonder scaffold's height.
He will be known !   He will be known !

> [*Bowing courteously, with a word to his
> Indian companion, he moves through the
> crowd towards the scaffold.   The gov-
> ernor of the State, Magistrates, Clergy-
> men ; among them the* REV. FATHER
> WILSON *old and stern, and* MR. DIM-
> MESDALE.   *They sit in a balcony above
> the scaffold.*

WILSON.

Hearken unto me, Hester Prynne !
I have striven with my young brother,

> [*Lays his hand on* MR. DIMMESDALE'S
> shoulder.*

I have sought and do persuade
This godly youth he deal with you
Here in the face of heaven
And these honest upright people.
I do entreat he speak to you
Upon the vileness of your sin.
Knowing your natural temper
Better far than I, he may the better judge
What argument to use, of tenderness or terror,
As might prevail against your hardness.
Insomuch you do no longer
Hide the partner of your shame.
But he denies me with his over-softness, —

Albeit wise beyond his years, —
And says it wrongs the very nature of the woman
To force her bare her bosom's secret
To the day's broad light and the assembled multitude.
I have sought to prove the sin lay in commission,
Not in showing forth.
What say, once again, my brother Dimmesdale? —
Shall it be you, or I, that deal with this poor sinner's
      soul?

Gov. Bellingham.

Most worthy Master Dimmesdale,
This woman's soul lies well with you
Her pastor and adviser:
It behooves you to exhort her to repent, —
Confess as proof and consequence thereof.

Wilson.

My brother, speak unto this woman!
'Tis of moment to her soul:
Our most worshipful governor says,
Momentous to thine own, who hold this charge:
Exhort her to the truth!

Dimmesdale.

Hester Prynne, thou hearest what this good man
      sayest,
Thou seest how great mine own accountability.
If it be for thy soul's peace
And that thy earthly punishment

Be effectual to salvation,
I charge thee speak out thy fellow-sinner's,
Thy fellow-sufferer's name.
Have no mistaken pity !
Hester, believe me, did he step
From high places to thy pedestal of shame,
It were better so than struggle with a sin
That, unatoned by free confession,
Would sap the strength of life,
And prey upon the vital spark
Till the maddened soul within
Would rush in vain remorse
To suicidal death and hell's enduring flames.
Thy silence wrongs him,
Yea, compels him to sin.
Thou hast been granted open ignominy :
Thou mayest work out an open triumph over evil.
Take heed that thou deny him not
Who mayhap is too weak, too sinful weak,
To clasp that bitter but unwholesome cup
Thou drainest to revolting lees.
I do implore thee, speak !

       [HESTER *shakes her head in denial.*

WILSON.

Woman ! know you not that Heaven
Has limits to its mercy ?
Thy little babe does still confirm
The counsel thou hast heard,
Yet, godless, hast not heeded.

Speak out the name !
That and thy repentance may avail
To take the Scarlet Letter off thy breast.

HESTER.

Never ! Ye cannot take it off!
Do ye not know that this red infamy
[*Puts her hand on the letter*] Is branded in my soul ?
Nought save the grave's chill dust
Can fade the hue and color of my misery !
I speak his name, condemn to shame —
When, all the long night through,
I pray the mighty, the forgiving Father,
To grant my sinfulness the power
To bear his agony, nor heed mine own !

ROGER.

Speak, woman, speak !
And give thy child a father.

HESTER.

I will not speak !
She may not know an earthly father;
But I will strive to early teach
My sin-born child to seek a heavenly one.

WILSON.

Once again I do command thou speakest!

3

HESTER.

Vain are thy words !   I will not speak !
Condemned, lost, I still do hold
My womanhood with all its heritage of grief.
Ye may hang me till my struggling members
Still in death ; ye may torture
By rack and flame :
Ye cannot make me speak
Nor bare the breast whose outward symbol
Speaks of blackest misery :
Ay, women ! grievously fallen though I be,
I yet do hold in common with ye
The power to suffer and be still.

ACT II.

SCENE I. — *Night.* ROGER CHILLINGWORTH, *at the door of* HESTER'S *prison, speaks with the Jailer.*

ROGER CHILLINGWORTH.

Prithee, good friend, leave me here awhile:
Esculapius' art I bring.   I promise thee
Mistress Prynne shall be more amenable
Than thou hast found her heretofore.

BEROCKET.

Nay! if your worship do but accomplish that,
I will own you for a man of skill indeed.
Verily the woman has been like one possessed;
And little lack I take the lash
To drive out Satan.

SCENE II. — *He enters ; approaches a bed where the child lies moaning.   Scanning it carefully, he unclasps a leathern case from his person, containing medicine ; one of which he mingles with water.*

ROGER CHILLINGWORTH.

My knowledge of alchemy, and sojourn with a people

Versed in properties of simples, have made me a
    physician
Better than many that claim degrees.
Here, woman, this child is yours;
She is none of mine:
Give her the draught with thine own hand.

HESTER.

Wouldst thou poison my innocent babe?

ROGER CHILLINGWORTH (*half soothingly*).

Foolish woman!
Would I harm this misbegotten wretched babe?
The medicine is potent for good.
Were it my child and thine,
I could no better do.
> [*He administers the potion. The child sleeps.
> Steps to* HESTER'S *side, touches her pulse,
> and offers the cup. She draws back shud-
> deringly.*

ROGER CHILLINGWORTH.

I give not Lethe nor Nepenthe.
'Tis a potion taught me by an Indian
In return for lessons of mine own,
Old, old as Paracelsus.
Drink.   (*Presenting the cup.*)
'Twill calm the swell and heaving of thy passions.

HESTER.

I have thought of death, — prayed for it.

Yet, if death's oblivion sleep within this cup,
I bid thee think again
Ere thou bidst me quaff.
See, e'en now, I drink.

Roger Chillingworth.

Dost thou know me so little, Hester Prynne?
Are my purposes so shallow?
What scheme of vengeance do I perpetrate
If I give thee o'er to death?
For death be rest and peace;
And life be torture and endurance.
Ay, live to bear thy blazing shame.
                    [*Lays his finger on the letter.*
Live to bear thy doom
In the eyes of scorning men and women,
In the eyes of him thou callest husband,
In the eyes of yonder child.

Hester.

Why taunt me with my infamy?
Hath not my sin found me out?
Lies not my future black and wasted?
Its passions dead and soulless, save
The pure springs of mother-love,
That, welling from a fountain foul,
Shall taint my one lone joy?

Roger Chillingworth.

Here, drink that thou mayest live.

[*She drinks at his motion ; sits on the child's
bed.   He draws up the only chair in the
room, and sits near her.   She trembles.*

Hester, I do not ask wherefore or how
Thou fell into this pit ;
Or, rather, mounted to that pinnacle of shame
On which I found thee.
My folly and thy weakness !
I, a bookworm of great libraries,
Old, misshapen from my birth, —
How dared I mate with youth and beauty
Like thine own ?
Nay, when we walked from the old church down,
Had I been wise, I might have seen
The baleful glare of thy scarlet shame.

HESTER.

Thou knowest I did not feign to love thee.
I gave no pretence of a passion
That to my undeveloped nature had not form.
In childish trust I gave my hand to thee.
Thou wert my one friend :
My heart knew tender reverence,
But gave no quick response to thy strong passions.

ROGER CHILLINGWORTH.

Later, and to thy ruin, self-knowledge came.

HESTER.

To my ruin there came a day
When the free hand trembled at a touch

That thrilled my soul to life;
I woke to full conception of a world
Centred in one human life.
I woke to the revelation of my being;
And my untaught instincts cried out, —
What might I bestow upon my king!
I longed for sacrifice, that should speak
The worship that bound my will.
Why do I speak of a past
Whose days held within their fleeting span,
Such fulness of joy, of rapture,
That when the night came down,
Devastating the memory of my bliss,
I seemed within my grave?
With dulled brain and groping hands,
I reached out to life again.
Remorse and deadly fear encompassed me;
I lay within the grave of infamy.
Why didst thou send me from thee?
Why didst thou wed me?

ROGER CHILLINGWORTH.

True, true; it was my folly,
But till that epoch of life
I seeming lived in vain.
The world had been so cheerless,
My heart held habitation for many guests,
And longed for cheer of household flame.
It was a wild dream;
Old as I was, misshapen, grave,

I hoped the simple bliss
Which scattered far and wide,
All mankind may gather up, might yet be mine;
And, Hester, in my heart I drew thee,
And sought to warm thee
By the joy thy presence gave.

HESTER.

I have most cruel wronged thee.

ROGER CHILLINGWORTH.

We have wronged each other. Mine was the first
When I betrayed thy budding youth
In most unnatural union with decay.
As one who has not philosophized in vain,
I take no thought of vengeance 'gainst thee:
Between thee and me the scales are fairly balanced.
But, Hester, he who has wronged us both,
Speak out his name!

HESTER.

Thou shalt never know.

ROGER CHILLINGWORTH.

Never, sayest thou? Believe me, I shall know:
Cover thy secret as thou mayest,
I shall seek this man
As men seek truth in books,
Or gold in alchemy.
There will come a sympathy

That shall speak his presence.
Sooner or later he needs must be mine.
Thou wilt not speak, none the less he be mine.
His garments bear no mark of infamy;
But I shall read his soul.
I judge him for a man of fair repute,
Ay; start not:
I will not lead him to the grip of human law;
Let all outward honors compass him,
I will uphold them, and leave him with his conscience:
Yet none the less be he mine.

HESTER.

Thy words are merciful,
And yet they hold within them terror.

ROGER CHILLINGWORTH.

Thou hast well kept the secret of thy paramour:
Keep likewise mine. Thou wert my wife:
Speak not to any human soul
That thou didst ever call me husband.
Wanderer as I am, and isolated from all human ties.
Here will I pitch my tent;
For thou and thine are mine.
What matter the ligaments be love or hate?
My home is where thou art and thy sin's abettor.
Betray me not!

HESTER.

Wherefore? I like not this secret bond;
Openly announce thyself, and cast me off.

4

Roger Chillingworth.

Shall I tell thee ?   I will not meet dishonor
That besmirches the husband of a faithless wife;
Enough. I would live and die unknown.
Thy husband is as one dead,
From whom no tidings ever come.
Know me not by word, or sign, or look ;
Breathe not the secret to the man thou wottest of.
Shouldst thou deceive me,
His life, his fame, be in my hands.   Beware !

Hester.

I will not speak thy name or mission.

Roger Chllingworth.

Swear it.   [*She kisses the Bible, and swears.*
[*Sarcastically.*]   Mistress Prynne, I leave thee
With thy child, thy Scarlet Letter,
And thy pleasant retrospections ;
Doth thy sentence bind thee
To wear e'en in thy sleep thy scarlet symbol ?
Art thou not in terror of black dreams and nightmare ?

Hester.

Why dost thou smile on me ?
Thy levity seemeth evil.
Hast thou enticed me in a bond
That shall ruin quite my sinful soul ?

Roger Chillingworth.

Not thy soul ; no, not thy soul.

[*Exit* Roger.

HESTER.

Betray him!
The grief that rends my dishonored breast
Is that I may not bear his agony.

> [*Sits down at the table ; opening the Bible,
> reads from the Apocrypha.*

Oh ! Judith mourned not more her crime
Or deed, than I mourn the life I loved
To fill with lengthened vain remorse.

> [*Reads again, and, looking away, sits
> thoughtful.*

To break from bonding thrall the people that she
    loved,
To bid the fainting hearts of women cheer and hope,
To strengthen manly arms to deeds of valor and of
    fame,
She trailed the whitened purity of robes unstained
By envy's cruel thrust, undefiled by lust or shame,
In lecherous pools of royal blood.
Bowed, crushed, she loathed the beauty
That in her puny hand
An instrument of vengeance God had made ;
Threading with quivering fingers
The shadowing darkness of her hair,
As if the ashes of atonement, poured upon her heart,
Had drifted o'er the soft luxuriance,
And left its splendor blanched to whiteness.
Deeds of death, and trust betrayed, change not the
    face.
Judith's face be fair, and eyes as winsome

As when their pleading softness lured the heart
Of Holofernes, — lured him to trust and death.
It is a shuddering thing to smile and soothe
With lovingness till gentle sleep shall come,
And, looking on the still face, strike to death.
O Judith ! this was thy deed, — dark, revolting in its
        truth,
Yet great, heroic in its purpose.
To give thyself to evil, to sacrifice thyself
That thy people's wrongs might know redress,
Doth sanctify thee.   I had no wrongs.   (*Weeps.*)
I would not weep did I not love the man
Into whose white life I crept, to give him pain and
        sorrow.
To gaze into the eyes that always smiled on me,
To listen to the voice so soft and tender
At my coming, was such sweet joy
That I forgot all else ; and, sinking down
Close in his heart, I made him dread
Communion with his God.
Oh, agony !   To know that I have banished
Peace and joy and sweet content from out thy life,
My Scarlet Letter burns. nor tortures less.
Accurst am I; destroying that
Which I most cherished.

> [*Enter Jailer.* HESTER *stands at the open
> window looking out : the moon is full,
> and shines upon her face and across the
> bed.   She does not heed his entrance.
> Whippoorwills are singing.*

Jailer.

Mistress Hester, how may I serve you ?
By my soul, I thought the woman
Meant madness or murder :
There she be as grand as any queen.
Truly these dark wimmen are curious.
       [He pauses, gazing upon her.

Hester.

Methinks the moon ne'er gave so soft a light,
It seeketh not my shame ;
It speaketh peace from its far purity,
And bids my impatient spirit rest.
For soon the blaze of day shall come
To drive me forth with my brand of Cain.
And never while heart shall beat,
And never while the sad soul agonize,
Shall I take mine own again.
Ever a thing despised and shunned.
A creature apart from honor and fame.

Jailer.

Ay, talk away to the moon :
It be death to a woman
If nothing listen to her complainings.
I would my old wife took the cue,
And talked to the moon and whippowils !

HESTER.

[*Goes to the bed, and bends over the child.*]
This much of life I yet have left.
My future holds but thee, my child.
[*Clasping it fondly.*
Within thy frailty lies the germ of immortality,
And I will struggle for thy soul,
Though fiends should compass thee about,
My babe, my nameless one.
I call thee Pearl, my priceless pearl :
Did I not purchase thee with my sole treasure ?
Sleep on, my innocent!
Too soon, too soon, to thy frail life
Will come the morn.   [*Gazing tenderly.*
My innocent!   I thirst to call thee ever thus,
For thou art innocent.   [*Kneeling.*
Heaven guard thee, sinless one of sin !

ACT III.

SCENE I. — *Room in* MR. DIMMESDALE'S *house.* MR. DIMMESDALE *ill, reclining on a couch.* DR. CHILLINGWORTH *attends him. An interval of six years supposed to have elapsed.*

DR. CHILLINGWORTH.

Honoring thee, and loving thee, thy people do en-
    treat,
I bring my leech's skill and healing lotions,
And tempt thee back to health again.
Art sick in body? or in mind opprest?

DIMMESDALE.

[*Turning his head wearily.*]
I want no healing lotion.   Did God will,
I were content to lay my labors down.

DR. CHILLINGWORTH.

Youthful men take not deep root on life,
And loose their hold at pain;
And saintly men who walk with God on earth
Fain would away to him, and tread the New Jerusalem.

DIMMESDALE.

Nay: were I worthier Heaven's eternal peace,
I were the more content to labor here.

DR. CHILLINGWORTH.

Good men do ever meanly hold themselves,
And heavy speak their own disparagement.

DIMMESDALE.

[*Taking some dark, rank leaves from the
doctor's hand.*]
Where, my good doctor, do you seek
Such black and noisome herbs?
Their very form and color doth offend the sense.

DR. CHILLINGWORTH.

E'en in the churchyard, quite at hand.
They grew upon a grave that bore no mark,
And did memorialize the dead.
They throve from out his breast, and do typify
Some hideous secret buried there,
That, unconfessed, they hold in black remembrance.

DIMMESDALE.

Perchance he did desire confession of his sin.

DR. CHILLINGWORTH.

And wherefore not?   E'en Nature calls;
And, from the black heart's buried shame,
Springs the rank luxuriance of unspoken crime.

DIMMESDALE.

'Tis but a fantasy ! If I forebode aright,
Nought save Divinity the soul may read ;
And I conceive that hearts that hold
Such blackening truths will yield them up
At that last day with joy unutterable.

DR. CHILLINGWORTH.

Why not reveal while yet in life,
And taste the solace of confession ?

DIMMESDALE.

They mostly do,
     [Grasping his vestments as if in pain,
And not alone when death its shadow throws,
And bids the soul cast off its wrappings, —
E'en while life be strong, and fame be sweet.

DR. CHILLINGWORTH.

Yet men do bury secrets black so deep,
God's mercy will not find them out.

DIMMESDALE.

Thy words do ring of truth. And yet, mayhap,
Kept silent by Nature's weakness.
Crime-stained their souls, they yet do hold
A zeal for God's high glory and man's well-being,
And trembling shrink to speak their crime,
Lest in the future be denied
The privilege to redeem by deeds of sacrifice.

3

DR. CHILLINGWORTH.

They do deceive themselves, and fear to take up
    shame
That should smirch or soil their earthly fame;
And love for man, and zeal for God,
Live not in hearts where guilt unbars the door
To hellish thoughts that propagate but sin.
Such unclean hands God's glory cannot build.

DIMMESDALE.

Let us not farther reason, but tell me of my body.
Speak, good friend and doctor, fairly,
Be it life or death!

DR. CHILLINGWORTH.

Fairly.   I do watch you daily;
And by the token of your aspect I do read
That in the soul the mortal sickness lieth.
Show me the wound that leecheth at thy life.

DIMMESDALE.

Nay! not to thee, nor to a brother man, —
None save my God, who knoweth my infirmity.
But who art thou, that darest thrust thyself
'Twixt me and life and heavenly mercy?

DR. CHILLINGWORTH.

My prescience, it doth anger thee.
I leave thee to the night and memory.
        [*Exit* DR. CHILLINGWORTH.   MR. DIMMES-
            DALE *paces the room wildly, beating his
            breast.*]

DIMMESDALE.

How poor a thing is life!   How terrible
When twin terrors — remorse and pain —
Drive talons deep with every heart-beat!
Seven years has my soul in bondage died;
Seven years has this old man probed my wound.
I put the hot iron to my breast,
And deemed that pain would assuage its anguish:
Yet it stilleth not; ever it eats and eats,
As God's judgments the flesh devoureth.
I will no longer bear it; but forth
On the pillory's shameful height I'll cry my shame,
And bare my branded breast to a world
That joys that evil liveth.
          [*He goes quickly from the room.*

SCENE II. — *Night in the market-place.* MR.
    DIMMESDALE *stands on the scaffold.* REV. MR.
    JOHN WILSON, *an aged minister, passes by.
    He holds his lamp in front of him. The night is
    dark.*

DIMMESDALE.

A pleasant evening to you, Father Wilson!
Come hither: a cheery hour we'll pass together.
          [*He passes without seeing or hearing.*
Thus ever doth penitence remain afar!
I grasp and grasp, and phantom-like it flitteth
Forever and forever, my weakness to elude.

[*Hester and Pearl approach.*

Whom have we here?   Hester!   Hester Prynne!
        Are ye there?

Whence did ye come ?   What sent ye hither?

Hester.

Governor Winthrop lieth dead.
His robe I measured, its foldings laid,
And now am homeward going.

Dimmesdale.

Come up hither, thou and little Pearl.
Come up hither once again.   Hearken !
        [*Weird singing in the distance.*

Pearl.

'Tis the " Black Man " singing to his people
As they dance to the roundelay.

Dimmesdale.

What knoweth thou of things so evil ?

Pearl.

My mother's home and mine is in the forest :
The trees when they whispered taught it me.
Was it evil that set us thus apart ?
For no one passeth under
The blooms that shade our door.
Not even thou, who smile on the sick and blind :
Wilt thou never come, minister ?

DIMMESDALE.

What wouldst thou, child?

PEARL.

That thou shalt stand to-morrow noontide here
With mother and with little Pearl.

DIMMESDALE.

Nay, not on the morrow: another morn as well.

PEARL.

But thou wilt take my mother's hand and mine
To-morrow at the noontide?

DIMMESDALE.

Not then, little Pearl, not then:
At the Judgment Day. These hands so alien
Then shall clasp for heaven or hell eternally.

PEARL.

Nay, minister; I will not touch thy hand
If thou take not mine upon the morrow.

DIMMESDALE.

Peace, child. The daylight of this world
Our meeting may not see.
> [*A meteor passes through the heavens.* HES-
> TER *looks up.* MR. DIMMESDALE *shud-
> ders.*

HESTER.

The soul of the dead passeth to judgment.

[By the light of the meteor ROGER CHIL-
LINGWORTH *is seen approaching.* MR.
DIMMESDALE *points to him.*

DIMMESDALE.

Who is that man ?   I shiver at his glance.
Hester, dost thou know him ?   I hate him.
A nameless horror seizes me : my soul dies within.
When he does touch my hand in greeting,
His will be seeming soft, yet holdeth me as iron.
He delves into my mind, and speaks my thoughts.
What is my soul to him ?
Canst thou, with thy preternatural gift
Of quick clairvoyance, tell me, be he man or devil ?

PEARL.

Minister, I can tell thee.

DIMMESDALE.

Quickly, child, ere he comes !
     *[She mumbles in his ear, and jumps away
     laughing.*

DIMMESDALE.

Dost thou mock me ?

PEARL.

Thou wast not brave, thou wast not true :
Thou wouldst not take my mother's hand and mine
To-morrow at the noontide !

[ROGER CHILLINGWORTH *approaches.* MR.
DIMMESDALE *recoils, and* HESTER *averts
her head, as he nears the scaffold.*

DR. CHILLINGWORTH.

Pious Master Dimmesdale, can this be you? ·
Well, well-a-day! but books do make men mad.
Thou art not strong, and the night wind blows;
The sleet, it sifteth on my beard.
'Twill chill thy weakness nigh to death:
I pray you, let me lead you home.

DIMMESDALE.

How knewest thou that I wert here?

DR. CHILLINGWORTH.

Most worshipful Governor Winthrop died this night.
My skill I gave his parting moments:
I now am homeward bound;
And I do beseech thou goest with me.
Such night exposure thy lease of days does shorten,
And contumely on thy fame might bring.
The night doth wane: wilt thou come with me?

DIMMESDALE.

I will go with thee.
[*He walks away helplessly, dropping his glove
on the scaffold as he descends.* HESTER
looks after them.]

HESTER.

'Tis like a slave that followeth his master.
My hand, that claspt these shackles on, shall free him
From a bondage that drinks his life,
And maketh him as a babe in weakness.

PEARL.

'Tis the " Black Man " that carrieth off the minister!
He'll catch both thee and me
If darkness it do find us out :
Take my hand, and let us run.

HESTER.

I have no free hand, Pearl, to hold thine :
These wraps do fill them quite.

PEARL.

Give me the shroud : I'll clasp it close, nor lose ;
And let us run, for I do tremble in my fear.

SCENE III. — *Market-place. Townsman lifting the glove marked " Arthur Dimmesdale."*

FIRST TOWNSMAN.

What have we here where evil-doers stand for shame ?
Satan put it as a poor jest 'gainst goodly Master
          Dimmesdale.
Such pure hands as his may go gloved
Save when he deals with sin :
Then will he strip them off, nor spare himself.

Second Townsman.

Thou hast well said; a more exalted servant
New England has not known.

Third Townsman.

The holy man, he seemeth ill and dying.
This world of evil be not worthy
The touch of steps so saintly in their walk.

First Townsman.

I'll tender him the glove ; and he will say
A cleverness that we shall love to dwell upon.
When his pure notes are dead to earth,
Yet higher tuned to heaven's great anthems.

6

ACT IV.

SCENE I. — *A forest.* HESTER *sitting on a fallen tree.* PEARL *putting flowers and leaves about the Scarlet Letter on her mother's breast.*

PEARL.

Why wearest thou this Scarlet Letter
Just where the minister layeth his hand in pain ?

HESTER.

It is my doom. I may not put it by.

PEARL.

Will I wear a Scarlet Letter when I'm a woman tall ?

HESTER.

Heaven keep thee from so fearful a fate !

PEARL.

Why fearful ? I love the letter.
Didst thou cast it off, I'd not call thee mother.
It is a beautiful letter, — my mother's letter.

HESTER.

Away to thy play, my Pearl.
There cometh one that I would speak with.

[ROGER CHILLINGWORTH *approaches.* PEARL
*seizes her mother's skirts in fear, and
quickly releasing darts away.*

HESTER.

I fain would speak with thee!

ROGER CHILLINGWORTH.

Aha! Has Mistress Hester words for Roger Prynne?
Why, Mistress Hester, I hear good tidings —
Noble deeds — of you from high and low degree.
The worthy magistrates do say your Scarlet Letter,
With safety to the common weal, may now be taken
 off.

HESTER.

It lieth not in the pleasure of the magistrates:
Were I worthy, of itself 'twould fall.

ROGER CHILLINGWORTH.

Nay! Wear it, then, if it suit you better.
A woman may her own adornments choose.
In faith, you wear it bravely. [*Sneeringly.*
What see you in my face? Your looks be grave.

HESTER.

Something that would make me weep had I bitter
 tears.
Of Arthur Dimmesdale I would speak.

ROGER CHILLINGWORTH.

What of him? Speak freely!

HESTER.

When last we spake together, seven years agone,
Thou didst extort secrecy of me relating to our past.
As this man's life and fame lay in your hands,
I did yield compliance to your will ;
But not without misgivings did I bind myself.
Since that day no man so near as thou.
Your footsteps followed his ; beside him as he slept
You searched his thoughts ; you rankled in his breast ;
You clutched his life. He dies a living death, and
        knows you not ;
I permitted this, and acted false to one I should been
        true.

ROGER.

What choice had you ? My finger pointed to the
        man,
And could have hurled him
From the pulpit to a dungeon, thence the gallows.

HESTER.

It had been better so !

ROGER.

What evil have I done him ?
I tell thee, Hester Prynne,
A monarch's richest fee could not have bought
The care I wasted on this wretched priest.
But for my care, in torment would his soul
Burned out these many months ago.

He lacks thy spirit's strength to bear his Scarlet Let-
    ter.
Oh! I could a goodly secret tell: [*chuckles*
He breathes, and creeps about the earth,
And owes his paltry life to me.

HESTER.

Better he had died!

ROGER.

Thou speakest truly. Better he had died.
The Creator has not made a man more sensitive,
Conscious of an influence falling like a curse,
Dreading death, despairing life,
And haunted ever by the presence of an evil
That tortured his guilty soul with undying remorse.
His spiritual sense did cry, it was no friendly hand
That smote his heart-strings to sudden pain.
With the poor superstition belonging to his craft,
He deemed himself given over to fiends.
Truly he did not err;
For I, to whom belonged a tender human heart,
Became a fiend for his life's torment.

HESTER.

Hast thou not tortured him enough?
Has he not paid thee all?

ROGER.

No, no! Tenfold hath he increased the debt.
Remember me, as I did seem nine years agone.

E'en then, in the autumn of my days, — the early
    autumn,
All my life was made of earnest, thoughtful years.
Faithful to increase my knowledge of book-lore,
Faithful to the advancement of human weal,
No life more innocent.   Few lives so rich with bene-
    fits conferred.
Dost thou remember?   To thee I might seem cold;
Yet I cared little for myself, much for others;
Kind, true, and just, and constant in my love.
Was I not this?

HESTER.

All this, and more.

ROGER.

What am I now?   A fiend.   Who made me so?

HESTER.

'Twas I, not less than he :
Avenge thyself on me.

ROGER.

I have left thee to thy Scarlet Letter.

HESTER.

It has well avenged thee.

ROGER.

I judged me so.   And now, what of this man?

Hester.

I must reveal thy secret.
'Tis due the man whose bane and ruin I have been.
I shall speak, —I, whom this *letter*
Has disciplined to truth, and given prescience
Of evil in each nature, whose eye shall fall
Upon its lurid, ignonimous splendor.
His honors do grow ghastly in such companionship,
Their very emptiness do mock his spirit.
I will not bend to pray thy mercy ;
Do with him as thou wilt :
There is no good for him, no good for me,
No good for thee — nor little Pearl.   [*She weeps.*

Roger.

Woman ! I could well-nigh pity thee.
Thou hast great elements :
I pity thee for the waste of a great nature.

Hester.

And I do pity thee, — a just, a wise man,
Transformed by hatred to a fiend.
Wilt thou not purge it out of thee ?
Not for his sake, but for thy soul's sake.
There is no good for he or me :
We grope in maze of evil, grown of guilt ;
But for thee a priceless, God-like privilege.
Forgive ! and leave his further retribution
To Him who claims his just prerogative.

See ! I kneel.   [*Falls on her knees before him.*
I do implore thee : turn not away.

ROGER.

Peace, Hester, peace.   It is not granted me to
      pardon.
Ye who have wronged me are not sinful,
[*Laughs*] Nor am I fiend-like.   It is our fate.
It is the fruit of evil that grew
From the black blossoms thou held out.
Revenge is sweet; and I will drink
Its tempting chalice to the dregs.
I go my way.
               [*He walks away.   HESTER bows her face
               in her hands.   ARTHUR DIMMESDALE
               passes without.   Seeing HESTER, she
               calls to him faintly.   He turns slowly,
               as if dazed.*

HESTER.

Arthur Dimmesdale !

ARTHUR.

Hester ! Hester Prynne !   Is it thou ?
And art thou still in life ?

HESTER.

Even so, — if life it be,
To live apart from human sympathy,
To cross no threshold, save where

Death and shame my path have cleared.
Hast *thou* found peace?

ARTHUR.

None.   Were I an atheist, devoid of conscience,
I might ere this forget mine evil-doing.
God's very gifts do now become
My ministers of torment.

HESTER.

Thy people reverence give,
And thou great good have wrought.
Does this not comfort thee?

ARTHUR.

More misery!   I stand before my people,
And accept their honest reverence,
Yet fain would strip my soul, and
Take, instead, their scorn and loathing.
They look upon me as if the light of heaven
Were beaming on my face;
And, hungry for the truth, grasp at my words
As if the tongue of Pentecost were speaking.
I look within, and at the black pollution laugh
In bitterness and agony of soul,
And Satan laughs.

HESTER.

But does not penitence bring relief?

7

ARTHUR.

Penitence ? I none have had, else I would long ago
Stript off this garment of mock holiness.

      [*Touching his vestments nervously.*

Would I had a friend who ever at my side
Would hold my confidence ! — a friend
Strong and brave like thee, my Hester !

HESTER.

Such an enemy thou hast beneath thy roof.

ARTHUR.

What sayest thou ? An enemy beneath my roof?
What mean you ? Speak !

HESTER.

O Arthur, forgive me !
In all things have I striven to be true.
Truth was my one sole virtue. I held it fast, —
Held it fast through all extremity,
Save where thy good, thy life, thy fame,
Were put in jeopardy.
A lie is never good, e'en though death threaten.
Dost thou not read what I would speak ?
That old man ever at thy side,
Roger Chillingworth, he was *my husband.*

ARTHUR.

Thy husband ?   [*Sinks on the ground beside her.*
I might have known ; I *did* know.

Did not my heart recoil at sight of him?
The shame, the ugly horror of association
With one who daily gloated at my misery —
Woman, woman! thou art accountable for this:
I cannot forgive thee.

    [Despairingly she throws her arms about him,
      pressing his face against the letter.

HESTER.

Thou shalt forgive! Let God punish.
Arthur, you will forgive? I have borne much.
The seasons have come, with heat and cold,
But gave me nought save life.
I might not look on the morning's scarlet glory,
Nor gaze on the sunset's splendor,
Nor pluck the crimson trumpet's bloom:
For each in its brightness cried to me
Of shame and sin and obloquy.
Seven long years has the world frowned,
And heaven has frowned; yet I have not died.
Yet now I will not live if thou dost turn
And frown in gloom upon me.
Forgive me. I would die or live for *thee*.

ARTHUR.

I do forgive thee, Hester. May God forgive us both,
Sinners as we are! this old man be even worse
Than thou the wife dishonored.
And I the priest polluted.

Has he not desecrated the soul's sanctity ?
Thou and I ne'er did that.

HESTER.

Never, never !
And we did consecrate ourselves to faithfulness
When we believed this old man dead.
Hast thou forgotten ?

ARTHUR.

I have not forgotten.
  [*Takes her face between his hands, and looks
   long and tenderly.*
For one brief moment I would live to truth,
Forget the mockery of my life,
Forget the hollow pretence of its forms,
And, gazing in thine eyes so firm and sad,
Take lesson of their calm endurance ;
So precious are these moments
That I would garner up their peace,
And bind my soul to strength.
  [*After a moment's silence he springs up
   wildly.*
Hester, here is new terror.   Will he betray us ?

HESTER.

He loveth vengeance; I trust him not.

ARTHUR.

And I, can I live longer with this deadly foe ?
Think for me, Hester : thou art brave and strong :
Resolve for me.

HESTER.

Thou must dwell no longer with him;
Thy heart would die beneath his evil eye.

ARTHUR.

What choice remains, it were worse than death.
Would I might lie me down
These withered leaves among,
And rise not till the angel call!

HESTER.

Alas! what ruin hath befallen thee!
Thou wilt die with very fear.

ARTHUR.

Heaven's mighty judgment is upon me;
My conscience stricken in despair.

HESTER.

Heaven would show mercy
Hadst thou strength to seize it.

ARTHUR.

Be thou strong, my Hester;
Advise me as thou wilt.

HESTER.

Is the world so narrow?
Does yonder town compass the boundless universe?
Listen: I know a world remote from possibility
Of contact with the dust you shake from toil-worn
        feet, —

A land of soft, tender skies and limpid streams,
Of smooth sea, of broad forest arches
Where singing birds do soothe the soul to stillness,
A land of pleasant melodies and dreamy thought,
A land of bloom, of fragrance, of forgetfulness :
Come with me. Why linger ?
Behind thee the dungeon's shame doth threaten
Mayhap an ignominious death.
Thy manacled hands will vainly lift for mercy,
Hearts untempted be sternly locked,
And mercy cheateth not their bolts.
Come with me and little Pearl :
I yet will save thee.

ARTHUR.

It cannot be. Wretched as I am, —
Lost as my soul may be, — I dare not leave my post.
Unfaithful sentinel ! who knows that death
And shame shall end his dreary watch.

HESTER.

Thou art crushed with misery :
Leave this wreck and ruin. Begin anew.
Hast thou exhausted possibilities ?
Exchange this false life for a true.
I am weary of dissimulation :
When words of love thrill my soul,
I feign would speak them ;
When thou dost suffer, I would weep ;
In joy or grief be ever at thy side.

ARTHUR.

This has been my sinful dream ;
Tortured as my soul has been,
I could not banish the hope so dear
That in another land or life
Thou wouldst be mine.
Dwell not upon it ;
Born of sinful thought, the hope must perish ;
And thou must guard thy glance, thy smile, thy
    tears.

HESTER.

Smiles I never have,
Nor will I weep to betray thee
Wert thou dead at my feet.
But is there no life for us ?
I will not yield the future :
Thou canst make a name and place
In the great outer world.
Preach, write, act, do any thing but die :
Let us up and away !

ARTHUR.

Thou wouldst surely go with me, my Hester ?

HESTER.

Will the bond take freedom ?   Surely !
" Whither thou goest " I go ; " where thou diest " I
    die.

Arthur.

[Looking long and tenderly upon her.]
Nay, nay ! It may not be.   Thou hast repute
'Mong these godly Puritans, won through strife :
I may not thrice make wreck of thee !
My time be brief.   I wait to meet my scarlet brand.
Turn thy suffering patient eyes from mine ;
They hold me, and do agonize my soul.

> *[She bows her head.   He lays his hand upon it.*

This head so lowly bowed, so bitterly degraded,
Weareth ever to my sight a crown
Of meek endurance.   God keep thee !
Farewell, Hester.

Hester.

Gone, gone !   Hope hath perished in this hour :
Would that life might perish too !

> *[He walks away.   HESTER bends even lower moaning.   Sadly moments pass ; she rises, and calls to PEARL.*

Pearl !   Pearl !   I bid thee come.

> *[She comes ; and, clasping her mother's neck, they sit on a fallen tree.   The child takes her handkerchief, and dries away traces of tears on her mother's face.*

Pearl.

Thou didst weep : I saw thee.
The minister said, Wilt thou kiss me, little Pearl ?

Nay, nay!   Thou didst bring my mother grief;
And I ran to thee.   Nor did I kiss.

HESTER.

Thou shouldst not deny him.

PEARL.

On the morrow 'twill be a brave show:
I'll wear a dress of white; and do thou, mother,
Glad thy Pearl, and wear white garments too.

CURTAIN DROPS.

8

ACT. V.

Scene I. — *A New England holiday. The new governor takes up the duties of office.* Mr. Dimmesdale *preaches the election sermon. Great enthusiasm. The market-place. People waiting for the procession to pass. Music and rejoicing heard in the distance.* Hester *and* Pearl, *wearing white, stand near the pillory;* Mistress Hibbins, *regarded as a witch, near them, fantastically attired. They look toward the procession as it advances.*

Pearl.

Is that the minister, that kissed me in the wood?
How grand and tall he walks beside the governor!

Hester.

Hold thy peace, dear little Pearl.

Pearl.

Will he kiss me now before the people?

Hester.

Thou art a silly little Pearl; mayhap, mayhap —

Mistress Hibbins.

What mortal mind could well conceive
Yonder divinity ? That saint on earth,
His people term him ; and I must needs say
He hath a look etherealized ; hearken !
From his study forth he went chewing Hebrew texts,
With Scripture in his mouth into the forest ;
And who forsooth shall say
He danceth not the measure when Satan fiddleth ?
Can we tell who shall change our hands,
If it be an Indian pow-wow, or Lapland wizard ?
'Tis but a trifle when a woman knows the world :
What think ye ?

Hester.

'Tis not for one like me
To lightly talk of pious Master Dimmesdale.

Mistress Hibbins.

[*Shaking her finger at* Hester, *and grinning
    maliciously.*]
Fie, woman, fie ! Have I been so often to the wood,
And cannot tell who goeth there ?
Thou wearest openly, there be no question here ;
But the minister— Put down thine ear
That I may whisper thee. Listen :
The " Black Man " knows his servants signed and
        sealed,
And he hath a way of ordering matters,
When one is shy in owning to the bond,

That shall disclose it in open light to all the world.
What seeketh the minister
To hide with his hands upon his breast?

PEARL.

What is it, good Mistress Hibbins?
Hast thou seen it?

MISTRESS HIBBINS.

No matter, sprite.   You will see it one time or other.
They say, child, thou art of the lineage
Of the Prince of Air.
Wilt thou ride with me in the moonlight
To see thy father?   Then shalt thou know.

PEARL.

I have seen the minister in the wood
And in the air [*points to the scaffold,*
And yet I do not know.
I will not ride with thee in the moonlight,
Nor is my father a prince of the air.
　　　[*Townsmen precede the procession, and enter
　　　　the square.*

FIRST TOWNSMAN.

I did not deem that man
Such God-like powers could hold;
His softness springeth but from a soul
That lives in near communion with his God.

Second Townsmam.

It seemed an angel spake.
How wept the congregation!
> [*The procession fills the square.* Mr. Dimmes-
> dale *stands at the governor's side. The
> people crowd around him, shaking his
> hands, and congratulating.*

Third Townsman.

He illy holds himself erect.
Such purity would bear translation.

First Townsman.

Good Master Dimmesdale, but let me touch your hand.
Such eloquence fell not from mortal lips before.

Governor Bellingham.

Thou art a people's pride, a country's glory.
Heaven give thee back to health and strength!

Dimmesdale.

> [*He seems not to hear; breaks away from the
> crowd, and gropes feebly forward toward
> the pillory. They would assist him.*
[*Waving them back*] Touch me not, touch me not!
> [*He pauses in weakness.*

Hester.

Come hither! Come, my little Pearl.
> [Hester *and* Pearl *step forward.* Roger
> Chillingworth *springs to his side, and,
> catching his sleeve, would restrain him.*

Roger Chillingworth.

Hold, madman!   Wave back this woman;
Cast off the child.   All shall be well.
Wouldst thou bring infamy upon thy sacred faith,
And perish in dishonor?

Dimmesdale.

Ha, tempter!   Thou art too late:
Thy power is over.   With God's help I do escape.
       [*Extending his hand to* Hester.
Hester Prynne, in the name of Him so terrible, so
      merciful,
Come hither.
Thou art stronger than this wretched, wronged old
      man:
Come, Hester, quickly.   Aid me!
          [*She steps to his side, holding* Pearl's *hand.
          He leans on her shoulder.   Together they
          ascend the scaffold.*

Hester.

O my master! forbear!

Roger Chillingworth.

Heed her words, and save thyself!
What folly wouldst thou perpetrate?

Arthur.

Away with thine evil counsellings!
Let me speak and die. —
Hester, come nearer; support me to mine infamy.

*[Leaning upon her shoulder, they ascend the
scaffold.
The people are offended, and murmur that he
will have none to support him save this
woman.*
HESTER *speaks in low tones.*

HESTER.

Arthur Dimmesdale, hast thou forgotten
The sacrifice, the endurance of these many years,
That ye dare with one fell blow
Destroy the structure that time and painful care
Hath built upon a tottering frame ?

ARTHUR.

I do not forget.   With Death's sure approach
Comes a prescience of evil-doing unconfessed,
That holds my tortured soul
Till I shall speak in late atonement.

ROGER.

Hadst thou sought the broad earth over,
There was no place so secret, no place so high,
No place so low, that thou couldst escape me,
Save on this scaffold.

DIMMESDALE.

Thanks be to God, who led me hither!
[He trembles, and turning from ROGER *gazes
tenderly on* HESTER.
Is not this better than we dreamed of in the forest ?

HESTER.

I know not! know not!　Better —
Yea! so both shall die; and little Pearl —

DIMMESDALE.

For thee and little Pearl, be it as God shall order;
And God is merciful.
But, Hester, I am dying:
Let me haste to take my shame upon me.

> [*Supported by* HESTER *he stands erect, ghast-*
> *ly, dying.　In a voice of agony he cries*
> *out, —*

People of New England!　Ye that have loved me,
Ye that have deemed me holy,
Behold me here, the one sinner of the world.
I whom ye behold in the robes of priesthood;
I who ascend the sacred desk,
And turn my pale face heavenward,
Presuming to take upon myself to hold communion
In your behalf with that Most High Omniscience;
I in whose daily life you saw the sanctity of Enoch,
In whose footsteps you saw the gleam of heavenly
　　　purity;
I who have baptized your children;
I who have breathed the parting prayer
Above your dead, and broke the bread of sacrament,
I your pastor, whom ye did love and reverence, —
Am all unworthy, a pollution, a lie.
I stand where seven years —

> [HESTER *interrupts him wildly.*

HESTER.

In mercy to thyself forbear!
Hath sympathy, hath pity for my shame,
Made thee mad?   Let me go from thee!
Let the strong arms of thy brothers
Bear thee to thy home,
Where rest shall bring tranquillity.

ARTHUR.

Not till the end.
Lo! the Scarlet Letter which Hester wears.
            [*Pointing to the letter.*
Ye have shuddered at it.
It cast the lurid gleam of infamy about her,
But there stood one in your midst
Whom ye bowed down to, whose infamy ye saw not;
        [*He all but falls, but mastering his weakness
            uprises again.*
It was on him.   God's eye beheld it;
The angels knew it; the Devil knew it,
And fretted it over with the touch of his burning
        finger.
He hid it from men, and walked among ye
With a mien of a spirit mournful
Because so pure, in a sinful world;
Sad, because he missed and longed for heavenly
        fellowship.
He stands before ye dying,
And bids ye look at Hester's Scarlet Letter.
He tells ye, with all its weird horror,

'Tis but a shadow of what his own breast bears.
Stand any here who doubt God's judgment?
Behold! behold a witness!

> [*He tears open his vestments, and betrays on his breast a red wound ; smiling triumphantly, sinks down.* HESTER *supports him.* ROGER CHILLINGWORTH *kneels beside him.*

ROGER CHILLINGWORTH.

Thou hast escaped me! thou hast escaped me!

DIMMESDALE.

May God forgive thee! *thou* too hast sinned.

> [*He turns his dying eyes on* HESTER *and* PEARL.

My little Pearl, dear little Pearl!
Wilt thou kiss me? Thou wouldst not
In the forest; but thou wilt now.

> [PEARL *kisses him.*

PEARL.

I will kiss thee, for now thou art brave, art true,
And dost not fear to take my mother's hand and
mine.

> [PEARL *looks around upon the people and scaffold.*

Tis like a picture in my lesson-book, — the crucifixion.

L OF C.

DIMMESDALE.

It is the crucifixion, my child, of passion and pride.

PEARL.

And yet 'tis even like the transfiguration.

DIMMESDALE.

It is the transfiguration of a soul purified by sacrifice.

HESTER.

Shall we not meet again?
Shall not immortal life be ours together?
Surely! Surely! We have redeemed one another.
Thou lookest far into eternity
With thy bright dying eyes.
Tell me, tell me, what thou seest?

DIMMESDALE.

Hush, Hester, hush. The law we broke.
I fear, I fear that when we forgot our God,
And violated reverence for each other's souls,
It be henceforth vain to hope eternal pure reunion.
God knoweth, and he is merciful, —
Merciful in giving me this burning torture
By sending yonder dark old man
To witness and intensify my agony,
By bringing me before my people
To perish in triumphant ignominy;
Had either these been wanting,
I had been lost forever. Praised be his holy name!

[*The people take it up repeating,* —

PEOPLE.

Praised be his holy name!

DIMMESDALE.

Death's tide breaks over me :
God bless my people, their children, and thee,
My Hester.   Farewell! farewell!
    [*He dies; the people murmur with resentment,
    believing him guilty of some great crime.*

FIRST TOWNSMAN.

Some monstrous crime hath he perpetrated :
His conscience would not give him rest
Till he should give confession.

SECOND TOWNSMAN.

Had his past held no evil-doing,
He casteth shame upon the church
In seeking death in the arms of disrepute.

DAME B.

Do we not hold among us *virtue,*
That he make this bold extremity?

REV. MR. WILSON.

Ye are hasty in your judgment: an hour agone
Ye fell in worship to him who lieth dead.

Dame Hibbins.

True, true : in sooth the world it changeth ;
Yet many hold an evil closer than she
Who weareth the scarlet token.

Magistrate.

What commandment hath he outraged ?
I have it : a felon's garb he feared,
Else had he spoken ;
Or, hath he done a murder?

> [Hester, *who has supported the dead pastor,*
> *is relieved by the sexton. She rises ma-*
> *jestically at these words of blame ; a fierce*
> *grandeur pervades her mien. In thrill-*
> *ing tones of offended entreaty, she speaks*
> *to the people.*]

Hester.

Shame upon ye ! Do ye,
His people who did love and reverence,
Upbraid at this fearful moment ?
Forget the mad self-accusations
Begotten of the morbid imaginings
Of a diseased mind.
He hath done no wrong
That prayer and penance hath not wiped away.
The Master he served laid hands of purity
On the repentant Magdalen !
Hath *he* done worse ? Have I not repented ?

Do I not plead, that ye forgive me
The bitter shame I cast upon ye ?

Rev. Mr. Wilson.

We do forgive, and bid ye come among us,   ,
Into the bosom of the church
That so long pronounced thy banishment.

People.

Thou art more worthy — [*Pointing to their late
    pastor.*

Hester.

Would ye defame the dead ? —
Your pastor, in whose life of purity
Ye could not point at spot or blemish !
Ungrateful people !   Do ye forget he loved ye,
Loved your souls, and struggled for their salvation ?
        [*Kneeling, and taking the hand of the dead.*
Look upon him, dead in thy service !
This hand did break the bread of sacrament,
Did put the cup of life to your parched lips,
Hath lain in baptism upon your children's heads.
Oh ! he loved your little children,
In death he gave them benediction.
Recall his goodness, his labors,
Recall his tender chidings, his loving counsel ;
His heart was so great, so merciful !   [*She weeps.*
It pitied me, and it hath doomed him to shame.
Forgive him this ; give back your reverence ;
Forgive me in whose arms he died.

Rev. Mr. Wilson.

We do forgive thee, who hath
So well redeemed thyself.
In the name of the people, I command
That ye put off thy Scarlet Letter,
And come down among us as of yore.

People.

Take off the letter!

Hester.

Do ye his people bid me cast it off?
I have sinned; I have tasted the bitterness of death.
Yet I am forgiven from the great heart of humanity
Even as Divinity forgiveth.
Use again this beneficent power,
And tell me ye do forgive his madness,
That the pale face looking heavenward
Is thy beloved pastor!

Rev. Mr. Wilson.

[*Shaking his head gloomily.*] He is beyond *our*
    honor;
His judgment be passed at a greater tribunal:
Yet do thou cast thy Scarlet Letter.

Hester.

Never! Ever at my heart this infamy shall burn.
If the dead who loved my soul lies in dishonor,
I will live in dishonor, — meet punishment

That I have brought obloquy on heaven's pure servant.

Rev. Mr. Wilson.

Thou teachest us a lesson.
Thy faithfulness restores him to our hearts
As ever, — the beloved pastor whom we do mourn
In deep reverence, and hold in tender memory.

People.

[*The people sob, and cry out.*]
Take off thy letter! take off thy letter!

Hester.

Across the dead I clasp thy hands,
And from my breast tear my Scarlet Letter,
At the mandate of a just people.

Finis.